'At night, among the reeds on the bayou, Chicot could still hear the woman's wail, mingled now with the croaking of the frogs.'

KATE CHOPIN

Born 1850, St Louis, USA
Died 1904, St Louis, USA

These stories were first published in *Vogue* and other
magazines between 1892 and 1897.

CHOPIN IN PENGUIN CLASSICS

At Fault
The Awakening and Selected Stories

KATE CHOPIN

A Pair of Silk Stockings

PENGUIN BOOKS

PENGUIN CLASSICS

Published by the Penguin Group
Penguin Books Ltd, 80 Strand, London WC2R ORL, England
Penguin Group (USA) Inc., 375 Hudson Street, New York, New York 10014, USA
Penguin Group (Canada), 90 Eglinton Avenue East, Suite 700, Toronto, Ontario,
Canada M4P 2Y3 (a division of Pearson Penguin Canada Inc.)
Penguin Ireland, 25 St Stephen's Green, Dublin 2, Ireland
(a division of Penguin Books Ltd)
Penguin Group (Australia), 707 Collins Street, Melbourne, Victoria 3008, Australia
(a division of Pearson Australia Group Pty Ltd)
Penguin Books India Pvt Ltd, 11 Community Centre, Panchsheel Park,
New Delhi – 110 017, India
Penguin Group (NZ), 67 Apollo Drive, Rosedale, Auckland 0632, New Zealand
(a division of Pearson New Zealand Ltd)
Penguin Books (South Africa) (Pty) Ltd, Block D, Rosebank Office Park,
181 Jan Smuts Avenue, Parktown North, Gauteng 2193, South Africa

Penguin Books Ltd, Registered Offices: 80 Strand, London WC2R ORL, England

www.penguin.com

This selection published in Penguin Classics 2015
001

Set in 10/14.5 pt Baskerville 10 Pro
Typeset by Jouve (UK), Milton Keynes
Printed in Great Britain by Clays Ltd, St Ives plc

A CIP catalogue record for this book is available from the British Library

ISBN: 978-0-141-39853-2

www.greenpenguin.co.uk

MIX
Paper from
responsible sources
FSC
www.fsc.org   FSC™ C018179

Penguin Books is committed to a sustainable
future for our business, our readers and our planet.
This book is made from Forest Stewardship
Council™ certified paper.

Contents

Désirée's Baby

As the day was pleasant, Madame Valmondé drove over to L'Abri to see Désirée and the baby.

It made her laugh to think of Désirée with a baby. Why, it seemed but yesterday that Désirée was little more than a baby herself; when Monsieur in riding through the gateway of Valmondé had found her lying asleep in the shadow of the big stone pillar.

The little one awoke in his arms and began to cry for 'Dada'. That was as much as she could do or say. Some people thought she might have strayed there of her own accord, for she was of the toddling age. The prevailing belief was that she had been purposely left by a party of Texans, whose canvas-covered wagon, late in the day, had crossed the ferry that Coton Maïs kept, just below the plantation. In time Madame Valmondé abandoned every speculation but

the one that Désirée had been sent to her by a benefi-
cent Providence to be the child of her affection, seeing
that she was without child of the flesh. For the girl
grew to be beautiful and gentle, affectionate and
sincere, – the idol of Valmondé.

It was no wonder, when she stood one day against
the stone pillar in whose shadow she had lain asleep,
eighteen years before, that Armand Aubigny riding
by and seeing her there, had fallen in love with her.
That was the way all the Aubignys fell in love, as if
struck by a pistol shot. The wonder was that he had
not loved her before; for he had known her since his
father brought him home from Paris, a boy of eight,
after his mother died there. The passion that awoke
in him that day, when he saw her at the gate, swept
along like an avalanche, or like a prairie fire, or like
anything that drives headlong over all obstacles.

Monsieur Valmondé grew practical and wanted
things well considered: that is, the girl's obscure origin. Armand looked into her eyes and did not care.
He was reminded that she was nameless. What did it
matter about a name when he could give her one of
the oldest and proudest in Louisiana? He ordered
the *corbeille* from Paris, and contained himself with

what patience he could until it arrived; then they were married.

Madame Valmondé had not seen Désirée and the baby for four weeks. When she reached L'Abri she shuddered at the first sight of it, as she always did. It was a sad looking place, which for many years had not known the gentle presence of a mistress, old Monsieur Aubigny having married and buried his wife in France, and she having loved her own land too well ever to leave it. The roof came down steep and black like a cowl, reaching out beyond the wide galleries that encircled the yellow stuccoed house. Big, solemn oaks grew close to it, and their thick-leaved, far-reaching branches shadowed it like a pall. Young Aubigny's rule was a strict one, too, and under it his negroes had forgotten how to be gay, as they had been during the old master's easy-going and indulgent lifetime.

The young mother was recovering slowly, and lay full length, in her soft white muslins and laces, upon a couch. The baby was beside her, upon her arm, where he had fallen asleep, at her breast. The yellow nurse woman sat beside a window fanning herself.

Madame Valmondé bent her portly figure over

Désirée and kissed her, holding her an instant tenderly in her arms. Then she turned to the child.

'This is not the baby!' she exclaimed, in startled tones. French was the language spoken at Valmondé in those days.

'I knew you would be astonished,' laughed Désirée, 'at the way he has grown. The little *cochon de lait!* Look at his legs, mamma, and his hands and finger-nails, – real finger-nails. Zandrine had to cut them this morning. Isn't it true, Zandrine?'

The woman bowed her turbaned head majestically, 'Mais si, Madame.'

'And the way he cries,' went on Désirée, 'is deafening. Armand heard him the other day as far away as La Blanche's cabin.'

Madame Valmondé had never removed her eyes from the child. She lifted it and walked with it over to the window that was lightest. She scanned the baby narrowly, then looked as searchingly at Zandrine, whose face was turned to gaze across the fields.

'Yes, the child has grown, has changed,' said Madame Valmondé, slowly, as she replaced it beside its mother. 'What does Armand say?'

Désirée's face became suffused with a glow that was happiness itself.

'Oh, Armand is the proudest father in the parish, I believe, chiefly because it is a boy, to bear his name; though he says not, – that he would have loved a girl as well. But I know it isn't true. I know he says that to please me. And mamma,' she added, drawing Madame Valmondé's head down to her and speaking in a whisper, 'he hasn't punished one of them – not one of them – since baby is born. Even Négrillon, who pretended to have burnt his leg that he might rest from work – he only laughed, and said Négrillon was a great scamp. Oh, mamma, I'm so happy; it frightens me.'

What Désirée said was true. Marriage, and later the birth of his son had softened Armand Aubigny's imperious and exacting nature greatly. This was what made the gentle Désirée so happy, for she loved him desperately. When he frowned she trembled, but loved him. When he smiled, she asked no greater blessing of God. But Armand's dark, handsome face had not often been disfigured by frowns since the day he fell in love with her.

When the baby was about three months old, Désirée

awoke one day to the conviction that there was something in the air menacing her peace. It was at first too subtle to grasp. It had only been a disquieting suggestion; an air of mystery among the blacks; unexpected visits from far-off neighbours who could hardly account for their coming. Then a strange, an awful change in her husband's manner, which she dared not ask him to explain. When he spoke to her, it was with averted eyes, from which the old love-light seemed to have gone out. He absented himself from home; and when there, avoided her presence and that of her child, without excuse. And the very spirit of Satan seemed suddenly to take hold of him in his dealings with the slaves. Désirée was miserable enough to die.

She sat in her room, one hot afternoon, in her *peignoir,* listlessly drawing through her fingers the strands of her long, silky brown hair that hung about her shoulders. The baby, half naked, lay asleep upon her own great mahogany bed, that was like a sumptuous throne, with its satin-lined half-canopy. One of La Blanche's little quadroon boys – half naked too – stood fanning the child slowly with a fan of peacock feathers. Désirée's eyes had been fixed absently and sadly upon the baby, while she was striving to penetrate the threatening mist that she felt closing about her. She looked from her child to the boy who stood beside him, and back again; over and over. 'Ah!' It was a cry that she could not help; which she was not conscious of having uttered. The blood turned like ice in her veins, and a clammy moisture gathered upon her face.

She tried to speak to the little quadroon boy; but no sound would come, at first. When he heard his name uttered, he looked up, and his mistress was pointing to the door. He laid aside the great, soft fan, and obediently stole away, over the polished floor, on his bare tiptoes.

She stayed motionless, with gaze riveted upon her child, and her face the picture of fright.

Presently her husband entered the room, and without noticing her, went to a table and began to search among some papers which covered it.

'Armand,' she called to him, in a voice which must have stabbed him, if he was human. But he did not notice. 'Armand,' she said again. Then she rose and tottered towards him. 'Armand,' she panted once more, clutching his arm, 'look at our child. What does it mean? tell me.'

He coldly but gently loosened her fingers from about his arm and thrust the hand away from him. 'Tell me what it means!' she cried despairingly.

'It means,' he answered lightly, 'that the child is not white; it means that you are not white.'

A quick conception of all that this accusation meant for her nerved her with unwonted courage to deny it. 'It is a lie; it is not true, I am white! Look at my hair, it is brown; and my eyes are grey, Armand, you know they are grey. And my skin is fair,' seizing his wrist. 'Look at my hand; whiter than yours, Armand,' she laughed hysterically.

'As white as La Blanche's,' he returned cruelly; and went away leaving her alone with their child.

When she could hold a pen in her hand, she sent a despairing letter to Madame Valmondé.

'My mother, they tell me I am not white. Armand has told me I am not white. For God's sake tell them it is not true. You must know it is not true. I shall die. I must die. I cannot be so unhappy, and live.'

The answer that came was as brief:

'My own Désirée: Come home to Valmondé; back to your mother who loves you. Come with your child.'

When the letter reached Désirée she went with it

to her husband's study, and laid it open upon the desk before which he sat. She was like a stone image: silent, white, motionless after she placed it there.

In silence he ran his cold eyes over the written words. He said nothing. 'Shall I go, Armand?' she asked in tones sharp with agonized suspense.

'Yes, go.'

'Do you want me to go?'

'Yes, I want you to go.'

He thought Almighty God had dealt cruelly and unjustly with him; and felt, somehow, that he was paying Him back in kind when he stabbed thus into his wife's soul. Moreover he no longer loved her, because of the unconscious injury she had brought upon his home and his name.

She turned away like one stunned by a blow, and walked slowly towards the door, hoping he would call her back.

'Good-by, Armand,' she moaned.

He did not answer her. That was his last blow at fate.

Désirée went in search of her child. Zandrine was pacing the sombre gallery with it. She took the little one from the nurse's arms with no word of

9

explanation, and descending the steps, walked away, under the live-oak branches.

It was an October afternoon; the sun was just sinking. Out in the still fields the negroes were picking cotton.

Désirée had not changed the thin white garment nor the slippers which she wore. Her hair was uncovered and the sun's rays brought a golden gleam from its brown meshes. She did not take the broad, beaten road which led to the far-off plantation of Valmondé. She walked across a deserted field, where the stubble bruised her tender feet, so delicately shod, and tore her thin gown to shreds.

She disappeared among the reeds and willows that grew thick along the banks of the deep, sluggish bayou; and she did not come back again.

Some weeks later there was a curious scene enacted at L'Abri. In the centre of the smoothly swept back yard was a great bonfire. Armand Aubigny sat in the wide hallway that commanded a view of the spectacle; and it was he who dealt out to a half dozen negroes the material which kept this fire ablaze.

A graceful cradle of willow, with all its dainty

furbishings, was laid upon the pyre, which had already been fed with the richness of a priceless *layette*. Then there were silk gowns, and velvet and satin ones added to these; laces, too, and embroideries; bonnets and gloves; for the *corbeille* had been of rare quality.

The last thing to go was a tiny bundle of letters; innocent little scribblings that Désirée had sent to him during the days of their espousal. There was the remnant of one back in the drawer from which he took them. But it was not Désirée's; it was part of an old letter from his mother to his father. He read it. She was thanking God for the blessing of her husband's love: –

'But, above all,' she wrote, 'night and day, I thank the good God for having so arranged our lives that our dear Armand will never know that his mother, who adores him, belongs to the race that is cursed with the brand of slavery.'

Miss McEnders

When Miss Georgie McEnders had finished an elaborately simple toilet of grey and black, she divested herself completely of rings, bangles, brooches – everything to suggest that she stood in friendly relations with fortune. For Georgie was going to read a paper upon 'The Dignity of Labour' before the Woman's Reform Club; and if she was blessed with an abundance of wealth, she possessed a no less amount of good taste.

Before entering the neat victoria that stood at her father's too-sumptuous door – and that was her special property – she turned to give certain directions to the coachman. First upon the list from which she read was inscribed: 'Look up Mademoiselle Salambre.'

'James,' said Georgie, flushing a pretty pink, as she always did with the slightest effort of speech, 'we want to look up a person named Mademoiselle Salambre, in the southern part of town, on Arsenal street,' indicating a certain number and locality. Then she seated herself in the carriage, and as it drove away proceeded to study her engagement list further and to knit her pretty brows in deep and complex thought.

'Two o'clock – look up M. Salambre,' said the list. 'Three-thirty – read paper before Woman's Ref. Club. Four-thirty – ' and here followed cabalistic abbreviations which meant: 'Join committee of ladies to investigate moral condition of St Louis factory-girls. Six o'clock – dine with papa. Eight o'clock – hear Henry George's lecture on Single Tax.'

So far, Mademoiselle Salambre was only a name to Georgie McEnders, one of several submitted to her at her own request by her furnishers, Push and Prodem, an enterprising firm charged with the construction of Miss McEnders' very elaborate trousseau. Georgie liked to know the people who worked for her, as far as she could.

She was a charming young woman of twenty-five, though almost too white-souled for a creature of flesh and blood. She possessed ample wealth and time to squander, and a burning desire to do good – to elevate the human race, and start the world over again on a comfortable footing for everybody.

When Georgie had pushed open the very high gate of a very small yard she stood confronting a robust German woman, who, with dress tucked carefully between her knees, was in the act of noisily 'redding' the bricks.

'Does M'selle Salambre live here?' Georgie's tall, slim figure was very erect. Her face suggested a sweet peach blossom, and she held a severely simple lorgnon up to her short-sighted blue eyes.

'Ya! ya! aber oop stairs!' cried the woman brusquely and impatiently. But Georgie did not mind. She was used to greetings that lacked the ring of cordiality.

When she had ascended the stairs that led to an upper porch she knocked at the first door that presented itself, and was told to enter by Mlle Salambre herself.

The woman sat at an opposite window, bending over a bundle of misty white goods that lay in a fluffy heap in her lap. She was not young. She might have been thirty, or she might have been forty. There were lines about her round, piquante face that denoted close acquaintance with struggles, hardships and all manner of unkind experiences.

Georgie had heard a whisper here and there touching the private character of Mlle Salambre which had determined her to go in person and make the acquaintance of the woman and her surroundings; which latter were poor and simple enough, and not too neat. There was a little child at play upon the floor.

Mlle Salambre had not expected so unlooked-for an apparition as Miss McEnders, and seeing the girl standing there in the door she removed the eyeglasses that had assisted her in the delicate work, and stood up also.

'Mlle Salambre, I suppose?' said Georgie, with a courteous inclination.

'Ah! Mees McEndairs! What an agree'ble surprise! Will you be so kind to take a chair.' Mademoiselle had lived many years in the city, in various capacities, which brought her in touch with the fashionable set. There were few people in polite society whom Mademoiselle did not know – by sight, at least; and their private histories were as familiar to her as her own.

'You 'ave come to see your – the work?' the woman

went on with a smile that quite brightened her face. 'It is a pleasure to handle such fine, such delicate quality of goods, Mees,' and she went and laid several pieces of her handiwork upon the table beside Georgie, at the same time indicating such details as she hoped would call forth her visitor's approval.

There was something about the woman and her surroundings, and the atmosphere of the place, that affected the girl unpleasantly. She shrank instinctively, drawing her invisible mantle of chastity closely about her. Mademoiselle saw that her visitor's attention was divided between the lingerie and the child upon the floor, who was engaged in battering a doll's unyielding head against the unyielding floor.

'The child of my neighbour downstairs,' said Mademoiselle, with a wave of the hand which expressed volumes of unutterable ennui. But at that instant the little one, with instinctive mistrust, and in seeming defiance of the repudiation, climbed to her feet and went rolling and toddling towards her mother, clasping the woman about the knees, and calling her by the endearing title which was her own small right.

A spasm of annoyance passed over Mademoiselle's face, but still she called the child *'Chene,'* as she grasped its arm to keep it from falling. Miss McEnders turned every shade of carmine.

'Why did you tell me an untruth?' she asked, looking indignantly into the woman's lowered face. 'Why do you call yourself "Mademoiselle" if this child is yours?'

'For the reason that it is more easy to obtain employment. For reasons that you would not understand,' she continued, with a shrug of the shoulders that expressed some defiance and a sudden disregard for consequences. 'Life is not all *couleur de rose,* Mees McEndairs; you do not know what life is, you!' And drawing a handkerchief from an apron pocket she mopped an imaginary tear from the corner of her eye, and blew her nose till it glowed again.

Georgie could hardly recall the words or actions with which she quitted Mademoiselle's presence. As much as she wanted to, it had been impossible to stand and read the woman a moral lecture. She had simply thrown what disapproval she could into her hasty leave-taking, and that was all for the moment. But as she drove away, a more practical form of rebuke suggested itself to her not too nimble intelligence – one that she promised herself to act upon as soon as her home was reached.

When she was alone in her room, during an interval between her many engagements, she then attended to the affair of Mlle Salambre.

Georgie believed in discipline. She hated unrighteousness. When it pleased God to place the lash in her hand she did not hesitate to apply it. Here was this Mlle Salambre living in her sin. Not as one who is young and blinded by the glamour of pleasure, but with cool and deliberate intention. Since she chose to transgress, she ought to suffer, and be made to feel that her ways were iniquitous and invited rebuke. It lay in Georgie's power to mete out a small dose of that chastisement which the woman deserved, and she was glad that the opportunity was hers.

She seated herself forthwith at her writing table, and penned the following note to her furnishers:

MESSRS. PUSH & PRODEM.

Gentlemen – Please withdraw from Mademoiselle Salambre all work of mine, and return same to me at once – finished or unfinished.

Yours truly,
GEORGIE McENDERS.

2

On the second day following this summary proceed-
ing, Georgie sat at her writing table, looking prettier
and pinker than ever, in a luxurious and soft-toned
robe de chambre that suited her own delicate colour-
ing, and fitted the pale amber tints of her room
decorations.

There were books, pamphlets and writing material
set neatly upon the table before her. In the midst of
them were two framed photographs, which she polished one after another with a silken scarf that was
near.

One of these was a picture of her father, who looked
like an Englishman, with his clean-shaved mouth and
chin, and closely-cropped side whiskers, just turning
grey. A good-humoured shrewdness shone in his eyes.
From the set of his thin, firm lips one might guess
that he was in the foremost rank in the interesting
game of 'push' that occupies mankind. One might
further guess that his cleverness in using opportun-
ities had brought him there, and that a dexterous
management of elbows had served him no less. The

other picture was that of Georgie's fiancé, Mr Meredith Holt, approaching more closely than he liked to his forty-fifth year and an unbecoming corpulence. Only one who knew beforehand that he was a *viveur* could have detected evidence of such in his face, which told little more than that he was a good-looking and amiable man of the world, who might be counted on to do the gentlemanly thing always. Georgie was going to marry him because his personality pleased her; because his easy knowledge of life – such as she apprehended it – commended itself to her approval; because he was likely to interfere in no way with her 'work'. Yet she might not have given any of these reasons if asked for one. Mr Meredith Holt was simply an eligible man, whom almost any girl in her set would have accepted for a husband.

Georgie had just discovered that she had yet an hour to spare before starting out with the committee of four to further investigate the moral condition of the factory-girl, when a maid appeared with the announcement that a person was below who wished to see her.

'A person? Surely not a visitor at this hour?'

'I left her in the hall, miss, and she says her name is Mademoiselle Sal-Sal – '

'Oh, yes! Ask her to kindly walk up to my room, and show her the way, please, Hannah.'

Mademoiselle Salambre came in with a sweep of skirts that bristled defiance, and a poise of the head that was aggressive in its backward tilt. She seated herself, and with an air of challenge waited to be questioned or addressed.

Georgie felt at ease amid her own familiar surroundings. While she made some idle tracings with a pencil upon a discarded envelope, she half turned to say:

'This visit of yours is very surprising, madam, and wholly useless. I suppose you guess my motive in recalling my work, as I have done.'

'Maybe I do, and maybe I do not, Mees McEndairs,' replied the woman, with an impertinent uplifting of the eyebrows.

Georgie felt the same shrinking which had overtaken her before in the woman's presence. But she knew her duty, and from that there was no shrinking.

'You must be made to understand, madam, that there is a right way to live, and that there is a wrong way,' said Georgie with more condescension than she knew. 'We cannot defy God's laws with impunity, and without incurring His displeasure. But in His infinite justice and mercy He offers forgiveness, love and protection to those who turn away from evil and repent. It is for each of us to follow the divine way as well as may be. And I am only humbly striving to do His will.'

'A most charming sermon, Mees McEndairs!' mademoiselle interrupted with a nervous laugh; 'it seems a great pity to waste it upon so small an audience. And it grieves me, I cannot express, that I have not the time to remain and listen to its close.'

She arose and began to talk volubly, swiftly, in a jumble of French and English, and with a wealth of expression and gesture which Georgie could hardly believe was natural, and not something acquired and rehearsed.

She had come to inform Miss McEnders that she did not want her work; that she would not touch it with the tips of her fingers. And her little, gloved hands recoiled from an imaginary pile of lingerie with unspeakable disgust. Her eyes had travelled nimbly over the room, and had been arrested by the two photographs on the table. Very small, indeed, were her worldly possessions, she informed the young lady; but as Heaven was her witness – not a mouthful of bread that she had not earned. And her parents over yonder in France! As honest as the sunlight! Poor, ah! for that – poor as rats. God only knew how poor; and God only knew how honest. Her eyes remained fixed upon the picture of Horace McEnders. Some people might like fine houses, and servants, and horses, and all the luxury which dishonest wealth brings. Some people might enjoy such surroundings. As for her! – and she drew up her skirts ever so carefully and daintily, as though she feared contamination to her petticoats from the touch of the rich rug upon which she stood.

Georgie's blue eyes were filled with astonishment as they followed the woman's gestures. Her face showed aversion and perplexity.

'Please let this interview come to an end at once,' spoke the girl. She would not deign to ask an explanation of the mysterious allusions to ill-gotten wealth. But mademoiselle had not yet said all that she had come there to say.

'If it was only me to say so,' she went on, still looking at the likeness, 'but, *cher maître!* Go, yourself,

Mees McEndairs, and stand for a while on the street and ask the people passing by how your dear papa has made his money, and see what they will say.'

Then shifting her glance to the photograph of Meredith Holt, she stood in an attitude of amused contemplation, with a smile of commiseration playing about her lips.

'Mr Meredith Holt!' she pronounced with quiet, supressed emphasis – 'ah! *c'est un propre, celui là!* You know him very well, no doubt, Mees McEndairs. You would not care to have my opinion of Mr Meredith Holt. It would make no difference to you, Mees McEndairs, to know that he is not fit to be the husband of a self-respecting barmaid. Oh! you know a good deal, my dear young lady. You can preach sermons in *merveille!*'

When Georgie was finally alone, there came to her, through all her disgust and indignation, an indefinable uneasiness. There was no misunderstanding the intention of the woman's utterances in regard to the girl's fiancé and her father. A sudden, wild, defiant desire came to her to test the suggestion which Mademoiselle Salambre had let fall.

Yes, she would go stand there on the corner and

ask the passers-by how Horace McEnders made his money. She could not yet collect her thoughts for calm reflection; and the house stifled her. It was fully time for her to join her committee of four, but she would meddle no further with morals till her own were adjusted, she thought. Then she quitted the house, very pale, even to her lips that were tightly set.

Georgie stationed herself on the opposite side of the street, on the corner, and waited there as though she had appointed to meet some one.

The first to approach her was a kind-looking old gentleman, very much muffled for the pleasant spring day. Georgie did not hesitate an instant to accost him:

'I beg pardon, sir. Will you kindly tell me whose house that is?' pointing to her own domicile across the way.

'That is Mr Horace McEnders' residence, Madame,' replied the old gentleman, lifting his hat politely.

'Could you tell me how he made the money with which to build so magnificent a home?'

'You should not ask indiscreet questions, my dear young lady,' answered the mystified old gentleman, as he bowed and walked away.

The girl let one or two persons pass her. Then she stopped a plumber, who was going cheerily along with his bag of tools on his shoulder.

'I beg pardon,' began Georgie again; 'but may I ask whose residence that is across the street?'

'Yes'um. That's the McEnderses.'

'Thank you; and can you tell me how Mr McEnders made such an immense fortune?'

'Oh, that ain't my business; but they say he made the biggest pile of it in the Whisky Ring.'

So the truth would come to her somehow! These were the people from whom to seek it – who had not learned to veil their thoughts and opinions in polite subterfuge.

When a careless little newsboy came strolling along, she stopped him with the apparent intention of buying a paper from him.

'Do you know whose house that is?' she asked him, handing him a piece of money and nodding over the way.

'W'y, dats ole MicAndrus' house.'

'I wonder where he got the money to build such a fine house.'

'He stole it; dats w'ere he got it. Thank you,'

pocketing the change which Georgie declined to take, and he whistled a popular air as he disappeared around the corner.

Georgie had heard enough. Her heart was beating violently now, and her cheeks were flaming. So everybody knew it; even to the street gamins! The men and women who visited her and broke bread at her father's table, knew it. Her co-workers, who strove with her in Christian endeavour, knew. The very servants who waited upon her doubtless knew this, and had their jests about it.

She shrank within herself as she climbed the stairway to her room.

Upon the table there she found a box of exquisite white spring blossoms that a messenger had brought from Meredith Holt, during her absence. Without an instant's hesitation, Georgie cast the spotless things into the wide, sooty fireplace. Then she sank into a chair and wept bitterly.

The Story of an Hour

Knowing that Mrs Mallard was afflicted with a heart trouble, great care was taken to break to her as gently as possible the news of her husband's death.

It was her sister Josephine who told her, in broken sentences; veiled hints that revealed in half concealing. Her husband's friend Richards was there, too, near her. It was he who had been in the newspaper office when intelligence of the railroad disaster was received, with Brently Mallard's name leading the list of 'killed.' He had only taken the time to assure himself of its truth by a second telegram, and had hastened to forestall any less careful, less tender friend in bearing the sad message.

She did not hear the story as many women have heard the same, with a paralysed inability to accept its significance. She wept at once, with sudden, wild abandonment, in her sister's arms. When the storm of grief had spent itself she went away to her room alone. She would have no one follow her.

There stood, facing the open window, a comfortable, roomy armchair. Into this she sank, pressed down by a physical exhaustion that haunted her body and seemed to reach into her soul.

She could see in the open square before her house the tops of trees that were all aquiver with the new spring life. The delicious breath of rain was in the air. In the street below a peddler was crying his wares. The notes of a distant song which some one was singing reached her faintly, and countless sparrows were twittering in the eaves.

There were patches of blue sky showing here and there through the clouds that had met and piled one above the other in the west facing her window.

She sat with her head thrown back upon the cushion of the chair, quite motionless, except when a sob came up into her throat and shook her, as a child who has cried itself to sleep continues to sob in its dreams.

She was young, with a fair, calm face, whose lines bespoke repression and even a certain strength. But now there was a dull stare in her eyes, whose gaze was fixed away off yonder on one of those patches of blue sky. It was not a glance of reflection, but rather indicated a suspension of intelligent thought.

There was something coming to her and she was waiting for it, fearfully. What was it? She did not know; it was too subtle and elusive to name. But she felt it, creeping out of the sky, reaching toward her through the sounds, the scents, the colour that filled the air.

Now her bosom rose and fell tumultuously. She was beginning to recognize this thing that was approaching to possess her, and she was striving to beat it back with her will – as powerless as her two white slender hands would have been.

When she abandoned herself a little whispered word escaped her slightly parted lips. She said it over and over under her breath: 'free, free, free!' The vacant stare and the look of terror that had followed it went from her eyes. They stayed keen and bright. Her pulses beat fast, and the coursing blood warmed and relaxed every inch of her body.

She did not stop to ask if it were or were not a monstrous joy that held her. A clear and exalted perception enabled her to dismiss the suggestion as trivial.

She knew that she would weep again when she saw the kind, tender hands folded in death; the face that had never looked save with love upon her, fixed and grey and dead. But she saw beyond that bitter moment a long procession of years to come that would belong to her absolutely. And she opened and spread her arms out to them in welcome.

There would be no one to live for her during those coming years; she would live for herself. There would be no powerful will bending hers in that blind persistence with which men and women believe they have a right to impose a private will upon a fellow-creature. A kind intention or a cruel intention made the act seem no less a crime as she looked upon it in that brief moment of illumination.

And yet she had loved him – sometimes. Often she had not. What did it matter! What could love, the unsolved mystery, count for in face of this possession of self-assertion which she suddenly recognized as the strongest impulse of her being!

'Free! Body and soul free!' she kept whispering.

Josephine was kneeling before the closed door with her lips to the keyhole, imploring for admission. 'Louise, open the door! I beg; open the door – you

31

will make yourself ill. What are you doing, Louise? For heaven's sake open the door.'

'Go away. I am not making myself ill.' No; she was drinking in a very elixir of life through that open window.

Her fancy was running riot along those days ahead of her. Spring days, and summer days, and all sorts of days that would be her own. She breathed a quick prayer that life might be long. It was only yesterday she had thought with a shudder that life might be long.

She arose at length and opened the door to her sister's importunities. There was a feverish triumph in her eyes, and she carried herself unwittingly like a goddess of Victory. She clasped her sister's waist, and together they descended the stairs. Richards stood waiting for them at the bottom.

Some one was opening the front door with a latchkey. It was Brently Mallard who entered, a little travel-stained, composedly carrying his grip-sack and umbrella. He had been far from the scene of accident, and did not even know there had been one. He stood amazed at Josephine's piercing cry; at

Richards' quick motion to screen him from the view of his wife.

But Richards was too late.

When the doctors came they said she had died of heart disease – of joy that kills.

Nég Créol

At the remote period of his birth he had been named César François Xavier, but no one ever thought of calling him anything but Chicot, or Nég, or Maringouin. Down at the French market, where he worked among the fishmongers, they called him Chicot, when they were not calling him names that are written less freely than they are spoken. But one felt privileged to call him almost anything, he was so black, lean, lame, and shrivelled. He wore a head-kerchief, and whatever other rags the fishermen and their wives chose to bestow upon him. Throughout one whole winter he wore a woman's discarded jacket with puffed sleeves.

Among some startling beliefs entertained by Chicot was one that '*Michié St Pierre et Michié St Paul*' had created him. Of '*Michié bon Dieu*' he held his own private opinion, and not a too flattering one at that. This fantastic notion concerning the origin of his being he owed to the early teaching of his young master, a lax believer, and a great *farceur* in his day. Chicot had once been thrashed by a robust young Irish priest for expressing his religious views, and at another time knifed by a Sicilian. So he had come to hold his peace upon that subject.

Upon another theme he talked freely and harped continuously. For years he had tried to convince his associates that his master had left a progeny, rich, cultured, powerful, and numerous beyond belief. This prosperous race of beings inhabited the most imposing mansions in the city of New Orleans. Men of note and position, whose names were familiar to the public, he swore were grandchildren, great-grandchildren, or, less frequently, distant relatives of his master, long deceased. Ladies who came to the market in carriages, or whose elegance of attire attracted the attention and admiration of the fishwomen, were all *des 'tites cousines* to his former master, Jean Boisduré. He never looked for recognition from any of these superior beings, but delighted to discourse by the hour upon their dignity and pride of birth and wealth.

Chicot always carried an old gunny-sack, and into this went his earnings. He cleaned stalls at the market, scaled fish, and did many odd offices for the itinerant merchants, who usually paid in trade for his service. Occasionally he saw the colour of silver and got his clutch upon a coin, but he accepted anything, and seldom made terms. He was glad to get a handkerchief from the Hebrew, and grateful if the Choctaws would trade him a bottle of *filé* for it. The butcher flung him a soup bone, and the fishmonger a few crabs or a paper bag of shrimps. It was the big *mulatresse, vendeuse de café,* who cared for his inner man.

Once Chicot was accused by a shoe-vender of attempting to steal a pair of ladies' shoes. He declared he was only examining them. The clamour raised in the market was terrific. Young Dagoes assembled and squealed like rats; a couple of Gascon butchers bellowed like bulls. Matteo's wife shook her fist in the accuser's face and called him incomprehensible names. The Choctaw women, where they squatted, turned their slow eyes in the direction of the fray, taking no further notice; while a policeman jerked Chicot around by the puffed sleeve and brandished a club. It was a narrow escape.

Nobody knew where Chicot lived. A man – even a *nég créol* – who lives among the reeds and willows of Bayou St John, in a deserted chicken-coop constructed chiefly of tarred paper, is not going to boast of his habitation or to invite attention to his domestic appointments. When, after market hours, he vanished in the direction of St Philip street, limping, seemingly bent under the weight of his gunny-bag, it was like the disappearance from the stage of some petty actor whom the audience does not follow in imagination beyond the wings, or think of till his return in another scene.

There was one to whom Chicot's coming or going meant more than this. In *la maison grise* they called her La Chouette, for no earthly reason unless that she perched high under the roof of the old rookery and scolded in shrill sudden outbursts. Forty or fifty years before, when for a little while she acted minor parts with a company of French players (an escapade that had brought her grandmother to the grave), she was known as Mademoiselle de Montallaine. Seventy-five years before she had been christened Aglaé Boisduré.

No matter at what hour the old negro appeared at

her threshold, Mamzelle Aglaé always kept him waiting till she finished her prayers. She opened the door
for him and silently motioned him to a seat, returning
to prostrate herself upon her knees before a crucifix,
and a shell filled with holy water that stood on a small
table; it represented in her imagination an altar.
Chicot knew that she did it to aggravate him; he was
convinced that she timed her devotions to begin when
she heard his footsteps on the stairs. He would sit
with sullen eyes contemplating her long, spare,
poorly clad figure as she knelt and read from her
book or finished her prayers. Bitter was the religious
warfare that had raged for years between them, and
Mamzelle Aglaé had grown, on her side, as intolerant
as Chicot. She had come to hold St Peter and St Paul
in such utter detestation that she had cut their pic-
tures out of her prayer-book.

Then Mamzelle Aglaé pretended not to care what
Chicot had in his bag. He drew forth a small hunk
of beef and laid it in her basket that stood on the bare
floor. She looked from the corner of her eye, and went
on dusting the table. He brought out a handful of
potatoes, some pieces of sliced fish, a few herbs, a
yard of calico, and a small pat of butter wrapped in

lettuce leaves. He was proud of the butter, and wanted her to notice it. He held it out and asked her for something to put it on. She handed him a saucer, and looked indifferent and resigned, with lifted eyebrows.

'*Pas d' sucre*, Nég?'

Chicot shook his head and scratched it, and looked like a black picture of distress and mortification. No sugar! But tomorrow he would get a pinch here and a pinch there, and would bring as much as a cupful.

Mamzelle Aglaé then sat down, and talked to Chicot uninterruptedly and confidentially. She complained bitterly, and it was all about a pain that lodged in her leg; that crept and acted like a live, stinging serpent, twining about her waist and up her spine, and coiling round the shoulder-blade. And then *les rheumatismes* in her fingers! He could see for himself how they were knotted. She could not bend them; she could hold nothing in her hands, and had let a saucer fall that morning and broken it in pieces. And if she were to tell him that she had slept a wink through the night, she would be a liar, deserving of perdition. She had sat at the window *la nuit blanche,* hearing the hours strike and the market-wagons

39

rumble. Chicot nodded, and kept up a running fire of sympathetic comment and suggestive remedies for rheumatism and insomnia: herbs, or *tisanes,* or *grigris,* or all three. As if he knew! There was Purgatory Mary, a perambulating soul whose office in life was to pray for the shades in purgatory, – she had brought Mamzelle Aglaé a bottle of *eau de Lourdes,* but so little of it! She might have kept her water of Lourdes, for all the good it did, – a drop! Not so much as would cure a fly or a mosquito! Mamzelle Aglaé was going to show Purgatory Mary the door when she came again, not only because of her avarice with the Lourdes water, but, beside that, she brought in on her feet dirt that could only be removed with a shovel after she left.

And Mamzelle Aglaé wanted to inform Chicot that there would be slaughter and bloodshed in *la maison grise* if the people below stairs did not mend their ways. She was convinced that they lived for no other purpose than to torture and molest her. The woman kept a bucket of dirty water constantly on the landing with the hope of Mamzelle Aglaé falling over it or into it. And she knew that the children were instructed to gather in the hall and on the stairway, and scream and make a noise and jump up and down like galloping horses, with the intention of driving her to suicide. Chicot should notify the policeman on the beat, and have them arrested, if possible, and thrust into the parish prison, where they belonged.

Chicot would have been extremely alarmed if he had ever chanced to find Mamzelle Aglaé in an uncomplaining mood. It never occurred to him that she might be otherwise. He felt that she had a right to quarrel with fate, if ever mortal had. Her poverty was a disgrace, and he hung his head before it and felt ashamed.

One day he found Mamzelle Aglaé stretched on the bed, with her head tied up in a handkerchief. Her sole complaint that day was, '*Aïe – aïe – aïe! Aïe – aïe – aïe!*' uttered with every breath. He had seen her so before, especially when the weather was damp.

'*Vous pas bézouin tisane*, Mamzelle Aglaé? *Vous pas veux mo cri gagni docteur?*'

She desired nothing. '*Aïe – aïe – aïe!*'

He emptied his bag very quietly, so as not to disturb her; and he wanted to stay there with her and

41

lie down on the floor in case she needed him, but the woman from below had come up. She was an Irish-woman with rolled sleeves.

'It's a shtout shtick I'm afther giving her, Nég, and she do but knock on the flure it's me or Janie or wan of us that'll be hearing her.'

'You too good, Brigitte. *Aïe – aïe – aïe! Une goutte d'eau sucré*, Nég! That Purg'tory Marie, – you see hair, *ma bonne* Brigitte, you tell hair go say li'le prayer *là-bas au Cathédral. Aïe – aïe – aïe!*'

Nég could hear her lamentation as he descended the stairs. It followed him as he limped his way through the city streets, and seemed part of the city's noise; he could hear it in the rumble of wheels and jangle of car-bells, and in the voices of those pass-ing by.

He stopped at Mimotte the Voudou's shanty and bought a *grigri* – a cheap one for fifteen cents. Mi-motte held her charms at all prices. This he intended to introduce next day into Mamzelle Aglaé's room, – somewhere about the altar, – to the confusion and discomfort of '*Michié bon Dieu,*' who persistently declined to concern himself with the welfare of a Boisduré.

At night, among the reeds on the bayou, Chicot could still hear the woman's wail, mingled now with the croaking of the frogs. If he could have been convinced that giving up his life down there in the water would in any way have bettered her condition, he would not have hesitated to sacrifice the remnant of his existence that was wholly devoted to her. He lived but to serve her. He did not know it himself; but Chicot knew so little, and that little in such a distorted way! He could scarcely have been expected, even in his most lucid moments, to give himself over to self-analysis.

Chicot gathered an uncommon amount of dainties at market the following day. He had to work hard, and scheme and whine a little; but he got hold of an orange and a lump of ice and a *choufleur.* He did not drink his cup of *café au lait,* but asked Mimi Lambeau to put it in the little new tin pail that the Hebrew notion-vender had just given him in exchange for a mess of shrimps. This time, however, Chicot had his trouble for nothing. When he reached the upper room of *la maison grise,* it was to find that Mamzelle Aglaé had died during the night. He set his bag down in the middle of the floor, and stood shaking, and whined low like a dog in pain.

Everything had been done. The Irishwoman had gone for the doctor, and Purgatory Mary had summoned a priest. Furthermore, the woman had arranged Mamzelle Aglaé decently. She had covered the table with a white cloth, and had placed it at the head of the bed, with the crucifix and two lighted candles in silver candlesticks upon it; the little bit of ornamentation brightened and embellished the poor room. Purgatory Mary, dressed in shabby black, fat and breathing hard, sat reading half audibly from a prayerbook. She was watching the dead and the silver candlesticks, which she had borrowed from a benevolent society, and for which she held herself responsible. A young man was just leaving, – a reporter snuffing the air for items, who had scented one up there in the top room of *la maison grise*.

All the morning Janie had been escorting a procession of street Arabs up and down the stairs to view the remains. One of them – a little girl, who had had her face washed and had made a species of toilet for the occasion – refused to be dragged away. She stayed seated as if at an entertainment, fascinated alternately by the long, still figure of Mamzelle Aglaé, the mumbling lips of Purgatory Mary, and the silver candlesticks.

'Will ye get down on yer knees, man, and say a prayer for the dead!' commanded the woman.

But Chicot only shook his head, and refused to obey. He approached the bed, and laid a little black paw for a moment on the stiffened body of Mamzelle Aglaé. There was nothing for him to do here. He picked up his old ragged hat and his bag and went away.

'The black h'athen!' the woman muttered. 'Shut the dure, child.'

The little girl slid down from her chair, and went on tiptoe to shut the door which Chicot had left open. Having resumed her seat, she fastened her eyes upon Purgatory Mary's heaving chest.

'You, Chicot!' cried Matteo's wife the next morning. 'My man, he read in paper 'bout woman name' Boisduré, use' b'long to big-a famny. She die roun' on St Philip – po', same-a like church rat. It's any them Boisdurés you alla talk 'bout?'

Chicot shook his head in slow but emphatic denial. No, indeed, the woman was not of kin to his

Boisdurés. He surely had told Matteo's wife often enough – how many times did he have to repeat it! – of their wealth, their social standing. It was doubtless some Boisduré of *les Attakapas;* it was none of his.

The next day there was a small funeral procession passing a little distance away, – a hearse and a carriage or two. There was the priest who had attended Mamzelle Aglaé, and a benevolent Creole gentleman whose father had known the Boisdurés in his youth. There was a couple of player-folk, who, having got wind of the story, had thrust their hands into their pockets.

'Look, Chicot!' cried Matteo's wife. 'Yonda go the fune'al. Mus-a be that-a Boisduré woman we talken 'bout yesaday.'

But Chicot paid no heed. What was to him the funeral of a woman who had died in St Philip street? He did not even turn his head in the direction of the moving procession. He went on scaling his red-snapper.

A Pair of Silk Stockings

Little Mrs Sommers one day found herself the unexpected possessor of fifteen dollars. It seemed to her a very large amount of money, and the way in which it stuffed and bulged her worn old *porte-monnaie* gave her a feeling of importance such as she had not enjoyed for years.

The question of investment was one that occupied her greatly. For a day or two she walked about apparently in a dreamy state, but really absorbed in speculation and calculation. She did not wish to act hastily, to do anything she might afterward regret. But it was during the still hours of the night when she lay awake revolving plans in her mind that she seemed to see her way clearly toward a proper and judicious use of the money.

A dollar or two should be added to the price

usually paid for Janie's shoes, which would insure their lasting an appreciable time longer than they usually did. She would buy so and so many yards of percale for new shirt-waists for the boys and Janie and Mag. She had intended to make the old ones do by skilful patching. Mag should have another gown. She had seen some beautiful patterns, veritable bargains in the shop windows. And still there would be left enough for new stockings – two pairs apiece – and what darning that would save for a while! She would get caps for the boys and sailor-hats for the girls. The vision of her little brood looking fresh and dainty and new for once in their lives excited her and made her restless and wakeful with anticipation.

The neighbours sometimes talked of certain 'better days' that little Mrs Sommers had known before she had ever thought of being Mrs Sommers. She herself indulged in no such morbid retrospection. She had no time – no second of time to devote to the past. The needs of the present absorbed her every faculty. A vision of the future like some dim, gaunt monster sometimes appalled her, but luckily to-morrow never comes.

Mrs Sommers was one who knew the value of

bargains; who could stand for hours making her way inch by inch toward the desired object that was selling below cost. She could elbow her way if need be; she had learned to clutch a piece of goods and hold it and stick to it with persistence and determination till her turn came to be served, no matter when it came.

But that day she was a little faint and tired. She had swallowed a light luncheon – no! when she came to think of it, between getting the children fed and the place righted, and preparing herself for the shopping bout, she had actually forgotten to eat any luncheon at all!

She sat herself upon a revolving stool before a counter that was comparatively deserted, trying to gather strength and courage to charge through an eager multitude that was besieging breast-works of shirting and figured lawn. An all-gone limp feeling had come over her and she rested her hand aimlessly upon the counter. She wore no gloves. By degrees she grew aware that her hand had encountered something very soothing, very pleasant to touch. She looked down to see that her hand lay upon a pile of silk stockings. A placard near by announced that they had been reduced in price from two dollars and fifty cents to one dollar and ninety-eight cents; and a young girl who stood behind the counter asked her if she wished to examine their line of silk hosiery. She smiled, just as if she had been asked to inspect a tiara of diamonds with the ultimate view of purchasing it. But she went on feeling the soft, sheeny luxurious things – with both hands now, holding them up to see them glisten, and to feel them glide serpent-like through her fingers.

Two hectic blotches came suddenly into her pale cheeks. She looked up at the girl.

'Do you think there are any eights-and-a-half among these?'

There were any number of eights-and-a-half. In fact, there were more of that size than any other. Here was a light-blue pair; there were some lavender, some all black and various shades of tan and grey. Mrs Sommers selected a black pair and looked at them very long and closely. She pretended to be examining their texture, which the clerk assured her was excellent.

'A dollar and ninety-eight cents,' she mused aloud. 'Well, I'll take this pair.' She handed the girl a five-dollar bill and waited for her change and for her parcel. What a very small parcel it was! It seemed lost in the depths of her shabby old shopping-bag.

Mrs Sommers after that did not move in the direction of the bargain counter. She took the elevator, which carried her to an upper floor into the region of the ladies' waiting-rooms. Here, in a retired corner, she exchanged her cotton stockings for the new silk ones which she had just bought. She was not going through any acute mental process or reasoning with herself, nor was she striving to explain to her satisfaction the motive of her action. She was not thinking at all. She seemed for the time to be taking a rest from that laborious and fatiguing function and to have abandoned herself to some mechanical impulse that directed her actions and freed her of responsibility.

How good was the touch of the raw silk to her flesh! She felt like lying back in the cushioned chair and revelling for a while in the luxury of it. She did for a little while. Then she replaced her shoes, rolled the cotton stockings together and thrust them into her bag. After doing this she crossed straight over to the shoe department and took her seat to be fitted.

She was fastidious. The clerk could not make her

out; he could not reconcile her shoes with her stockings, and she was not too easily pleased. She held back her skirts and turned her feet one way and her head another way as she glanced down at the polished, pointed-tipped boots. Her foot and ankle looked very pretty. She could not realize that they belonged to her and were a part of herself. She wanted an excellent and stylish fit, she told the young fellow who served her, and she did not mind the difference of a dollar or two more in the price so long as she got what she desired.

It was a long time since Mrs Sommers had been fitted with gloves. On rare occasions when she had bought a pair they were always 'bargains', so cheap that it would have been preposterous and unreasonable to have expected them to be fitted to the hand.

Now she rested her elbow on the cushion of the glove counter, and a pretty, pleasant young creature, delicate and deft of touch, drew a long-wristed 'kid' over Mrs Sommers's hand. She smoothed it down over the wrist and buttoned it neatly, and both lost themselves for a second or two in admiring contemplation of the little symmetrical gloved hand. But there were other places where money might be spent.

There were books and magazines piled up in the window of a stall a few paces down the street. Mrs Sommers bought two high-priced magazines such as she had been accustomed to read in the days when she had been accustomed to other pleasant things. She carried them without wrapping. As well as she could she lifted her skirts at the crossings. Her stockings and boots and well fitting gloves had worked marvels in her bearing – had given her a feeling of assurance, a sense of belonging to the well-dressed multitude.

She was very hungry. Another time she would have stilled the cravings for food until reaching her own home, where she would have brewed herself a cup of tea and taken a snack of anything that was available. But the impulse that was guiding her would not suffer her to entertain any such thought.

There was a restaurant at the corner. She had never entered its doors; from the outside she had sometimes caught glimpses of spotless damask and shining crystal, and soft-stepping waiters serving people of fashion.

When she entered her appearance created no surprise, no consternation, as she had half feared it might. She seated herself at a small table alone, and an attentive waiter at once approached to take her order. She did not want a profusion; she craved a nice and tasty bite – a half dozen blue-points, a plump chop with cress, a something sweet – a crème-frappée, for instance; a glass of Rhine wine, and after all a small cup of black coffee.

While waiting to be served she removed her gloves very leisurely and laid them beside her. Then she picked up a magazine and glanced through it, cutting the pages with the blunt edge of her knife. It was all very agreeable. The damask was even more spotless than it had seemed through the window, and the crystal more sparkling. There were quiet ladies and gentlemen, who did not notice her, lunching at the small tables like her own. A soft, pleasing strain of music could be heard, and a gentle breeze was blowing through the window. She tasted a bite, and she read a word or two, and she sipped the amber wine and wiggled her toes in the silk stockings. The price of it made no difference. She counted the money out to the waiter and left an extra coin on his tray, whereupon he bowed before her as before a princess of royal blood.

There was still money in her purse, and her next temptation presented itself in the shape of a matinée poster.

It was a little later when she entered the theatre, the play had begun and the house seemed to her to be packed. But there were vacant seats here and there, and into one of them she was ushered, between brilliantly dressed women who had gone there to kill time and eat candy and display their gaudy attire. There were many others who were there solely for the play and acting. It is safe to say there was no one present who bore quite the attitude which Mrs Sommers did to her surroundings. She gathered in the whole – stage and players and people in one wide impression, and absorbed it and enjoyed it. She laughed at the comedy and wept – she and the gaudy woman next to her wept over the tragedy. And they talked a little together over it. And the gaudy woman wiped her eyes and sniffled on a tiny square of filmy, perfumed lace and passed little Mrs Sommers her box of candy.

The play was over, the music ceased, the crowd filed out. It was like a dream ended. People scattered in all directions. Mrs Sommers went to the corner and waited for the cable car.

55

A man with keen eyes, who sat opposite to her, seemed to like the study of her small, pale face. It puzzled him to decipher what he saw there. In truth, he saw nothing – unless he were wizard enough to detect a poignant wish, a powerful longing that the cable car would never stop anywhere, but go on and on with her forever.